HENRY

JAMES

PERCY

MEET ALL THESE FRIENDS IN BUZZ BOOKS:

Thomas the Tank Engine
The Animals of Farthing Wood
Biker Mice From Mars
James Bond Junior
Fireman Sam
Joshua Jones
Rupert
Babar

First published in Great Britain 1992
by Buzz Books, an imprint of Reed Children's Books
Michelin House, 81 Fulham Road, London SW3 6RB
and Auckland, Melbourne, Singapore and Toronto

Reprinted 1993 (twice)

ISBN 1 85591 224 4

Printed in Italy by LEGO

THE TROUBLE WITH MUD

buzz books

One morning Thomas was being cleaned when Gordon arrived. Mud had blown all over his smart blue paint.

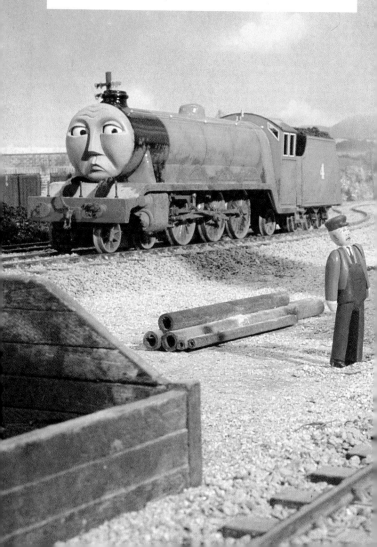

"Hello Gordon," called Thomas.
"You look as if you've had a mudbath.
Be a sensible engine. Have a shower
instead."

Gordon snorted. "I haven't time to dawdle over my appearance like fussy tank engines do."

The wind blew stronger.

"Whew Gordon, slow down," called his driver.

This made Gordon even crosser.

"I'll be dirty and late, dirty and late,"
he hissed.

At the next station was a sign:
All Trains Must Wash Down Daily.

James had just finished being cleaned.
"Come on Gordon," said his driver, "you'll
feel better after a good hose down."

"Paah," said Gordon and angrily let off steam.

"You're a very naughty engine," said Gordon's driver. "Now James will need another shower. You'll have to wait your turn till later."

"Good riddance," huffed Gordon. "I'm far too busy to waste time with water."

He finished his journey safely and steamed into the big station.

The Fat Controller was waiting. So were
Gordon's coaches and the passengers.

"Goodness gracious," said the Fat Controller. "You can't pull the train. Henry will have to do it. Gordon, you'd better get cleaned straight away."

Gordon was soon being washed.

"Mind my eyes," he grumbled.

Then he pulled trucks for the rest of the day.

He bumped them hard. "That's for you - and you - and you."

"Trucks will be trucks," said James.

"They won't with me," snorted Gordon. "I'll teach them."

James got ready to take the Express when Gordon returned.

"Be careful," warned Gordon. "The hills are slippery and you may need help."

"I don't need help on hills," replied James huffily. "Gordon thinks he knows everything."

17

Earlier a storm had swept Gordon's hill, blowing leaves onto the track. Even though the storm had passed, the hill was still difficult to climb. James knew this.

The signal showed 'clear' and James began to go faster.

"I'll do it, I'll do it," he puffed.

Halfway up, he was not so sure.

"I must do it, I must do it." But his wheels
slipped on the leaves.

He couldn't pull the train at all.

"Help, help!" whistled James.

His wheels were turning forward but the heavy coaches pulled him backwards.

The whole train started slipping down the hill. His driver shut off steam, and put on the brakes. Then carefully, he stopped the train.

Gordon saw everything.

"Ah well, we live and learn. Never mind little James, I'm going to push behind."

Clouds of smoke and steam towered from the snorting engines.

"We can do it," puffed James.
"We will do it," puffed Gordon.

At last they reached the top.

"Peep, peep. Thank you. Goodbye," whistled James.

"Poop, poop," answered Gordon. "Goodbye."

That night, the Fat Controller came to see the engines.

"Please Sir," said Thomas. "Can Gordon pull coaches again now?"

"If you understand that having a wash down is essential to every engine then, yes Gordon, you may."

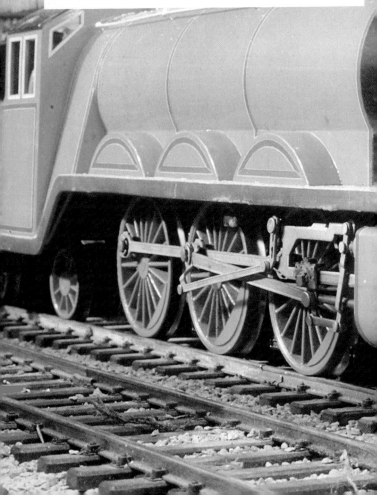

"Thank you," grunted Gordon.
The other engines settled happily to sleep.
"Dirty or clean, I'm a famous machine,"
murmured Gordon, but no-one heard
but him.

THOMAS

EDWARD

GORDON